W9-ADL-172

12/2015

WRITTEN BY JON SCIESZKA

CHARACTERS AND ENVIRONMENTS DEVELOPED BY THE

DESIGN garage

DAVID SHANNON   LOREN LONG   DAVID GORDON

ILLUSTRATION CREW:

Executive producer: TOR INDUSTRIES in association with Animagic S.L.

Creative supervisor: Nina Rappaport Brown ○ Drawings by: Dan Root ○ Color by: Christopher Oatley

Art director: Karin Paprocki

READY-TO-READ

SIMON SPOTLIGHT
NEW YORK   LONDON   TORONTO   SYDNEY

ABDO
Spotlight

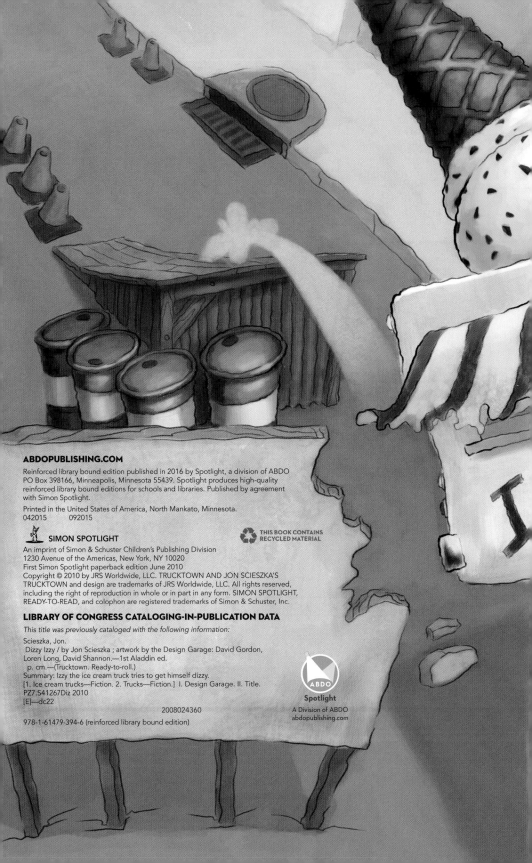

ABDOPUBLISHING.COM

Reinforced library bound edition published in 2016 by Spotlight, a division of ABDO
PO Box 398166, Minneapolis, Minnesota 55439. Spotlight produces high-quality
reinforced library bound editions for schools and libraries. Published by agreement
with Simon Spotlight.

Printed in the United States of America, North Mankato, Minnesota.
042015   092015

SIMON SPOTLIGHT

An imprint of Simon & Schuster Children's Publishing Division
1230 Avenue of the Americas, New York, NY 10020
First Simon Spotlight paperback edition June 2010

THIS BOOK CONTAINS
RECYCLED MATERIAL

LIBRARY OF CONGRESS CATALOGING-IN-PUBLICATION DATA

This title was previously cataloged with the following information:

Scieszka, Jon.
 Dizzy Izzy / by Jon Scieszka ; artwork by the Design Garage: David Gordon,
Loren Long, David Shannon.—1st Aladdin ed.
 p. cm.—(Trucktown. Ready-to-roll.)
Summary: Izzy the ice cream truck tries to get himself dizzy.
[1. Ice cream trucks—Fiction. 2. Trucks—Fiction.] I. Design Garage. II. Title.
PZ7.S41267Diz 2010
[E]—dc22
                              2008024360

978-1-61479-394-6 (reinforced library bound edition)

Spotlight
A Division of ABDO
abdopublishing.com

This is Izzy.

Izzy loves to get **dizzy.**

But is he?

Izzy gets
busy.

But Izzy is not dizzy.

Is he?

Izzy skids in a tizzy.
But Izzy is not dizzy.

Is he?

Izzy gets fizzy.
But Izzy is not dizzy.

Is he?

THEN IZZY GETS AN IDEA

Izzy whizzes.

Izzy fizzes.

Izzy gets busy and fizzy
and all whizzy
in a tizzy.

Izzy is
dizzy!

But
guess
what?